T0151598

Ross's

Personal Discoveries

Michael Ross

Ross's

Personal Discoveries

Michael Ross

Rare Bird • Los Angeles, Calif.

THIS IS A GENUINE RARE BIRD BOOK

A Rare Bird Book | Rare Bird Books
453 South Spring Street, Suite 302
Los Angeles, CA 90013
rarebirdbooks.com

FIRST HARDCOVER EDITION

Set in Minion
Printed in the United States
Distributed worldwide by Publishers Group West

Publisher's Cataloging-in-Publication data
Names: Ross, Michael, author.
Title: Ross's Personal Discoveries: Personal Relations: The Good, Bad, and Ugly/
Michael Ross.
Series: Ross's Quotations.
Description: First Hardcover Edition | A Rare Bird Book | New York, NY;
Los Angeles, CA: Rare Bird Books, 2018.
Identifiers: ISBN 9781947856868
Subjects: LCSH Books and reading—Quotations, maxims, etc. | Quotations, English. |
BISAC REFERENCE / Quotations
Classification: LCC PN165 .R67 2018 | DDC 808.88/2—dc23

To my family, friends, classmates,
shipmates, colleagues, students,
and other men and women
—you know who you are.

Introduction

Writing the introduction to my fourth volume of quotations is more difficult than it was for *Ross's Novel Discoveries*, *Ross's Timely Discoveries*, and *Ross's Thoughtful Discoveries*. In each of those, I endeavored, I hope with some success, to persuade readers of my qualifications for the quotes I selected and what I had to say about them. I also expressed some of the reasons why I believe quotations are important. In the hope that readers of this portion of my collection will have read, or will read, the first three volumes, I will try not to be repetitive.

I have an extensive collection of quotations on a variety of topics other than the ones contained in the first three volumes, such as life, death, fate, happiness, wisdom, communication, God, faith, religion, justice, law, and lawyers. I hope to offer additional volumes that will include quotes on these and other subjects. Nonetheless, I continue to read a great deal of literary fiction and collect quotes from my reading—the only source of quotes for my books.

The process of writing these volumes has had several effects on my reading. In an effort to offer quotes from different authors, I have broadened my reading to include books by many authors with whom I was not familiar, including some Nobel Prize-winners and other foreign writers. I think this volume includes about twenty new authors.

Another effect is the attention, which is sometimes a bit distracting, to searching for quotes worth sharing. I try not to let the quest restrict my selection of books, and there are many I read from which I find few or no quotes. I do, however, occasionally find myself thinking about the search as I read.

I also continue to look for literary fiction set in destinations for our travels. In recent years, this has included Melville's *Typee* and *Omoo* for French Polynesia, Balzac's *Père Goriot* for Paris, *Winter in Madrid* by C. J. Sansom in Madrid and *The Shadow of the Wind* by Carlos Ruiz Zafón for Barcelona, *The Spider's House* by Paul Bowles in Morocco, and for New Zealand *The Luminaries* by Eleanor Catton and *The Colour* by Rose Tremain. I find this practice significantly enriches the foreign experience.

The quotations here reflect some of the issues many of us face in our relations with strangers, acquaintances, friends, family members, partners, and spouses. Some people we know are loners, and, at the other end of the spectrum, others seem to know and be liked by everyone they meet. We see in others characteristics that bother or even repel us. We may, however, be less disposed to, or capable of, recognizing aspects of our own personality that impede favorable relations. We are sometimes conscious of playing a role professionally or personally, and there are probably situations in which we do it unconsciously. Some of us care more than others what others think of us, some people perhaps too much and others perhaps too little. Self-help books offer advice on how we might create better relationships. We read of medical research that suggests, or even proves, that favorable, close relations are healthy, especially as we get older. The one thing we share in common is our uniqueness, so there is no "one-size-fits-all" tailoring that will suit us for more and happier relationships. Nonetheless, these quotations may stimulate some productive contemplation of our relations and how we might appreciate the good ones and improve the others.

I cannot resist another mention of my fondness for quotes. The more I read and collect, the more I find myself recalling and trying to recite quotes in relevant conversations. This is not, I hope, an effort to show off, but rather to express understanding for what someone is saying. It occurs to me that quotes may be especially useful in our relationships. I hope that the quotes in my books will suggest some authors and books my readers have not read.

I also feel compelled to include my customary disclaimer about the selection of quotes in each section. There are numerous instances in which I moved quotes from one to another and, sometimes, back to the original section. I hope readers will not condemn me for my decisions; many quotes could rationally be in a different section. The same is true about inclusion of quotes in this volume rather than another.

Self First

The first person, and often the foremost person, in any relationship is oneself. Each person's character, experience, and perspective are critical in determining the nature of his or her relations with others. As some of these quotes reflect, for many people (at least in the fiction quoted), oneself determines, or at least strongly influences, the outcome of many relationships. Excess ego can make otherwise potentially mutually satisfactory relations difficult, if not impossible. Lack of knowledge of ourselves may also get in the way. Several quotes ask why we should pay attention to, much less focus on, others. Perhaps, the most provocative quotes are the ones that make us wonder just how well we know ourselves.

Although a family member may feel close to and like other family members, they may be consciously or subconsciously subordinated in importance. My favorite Canadian author uses an apt simile to express succinctly this notion.

«»

...One's family is made up of supporting players in one's personal drama. One never supposes that they starred in some possibly gaudy and certainly deeply felt show of their own.

Robertson Davies, Murther & Walking Spirits

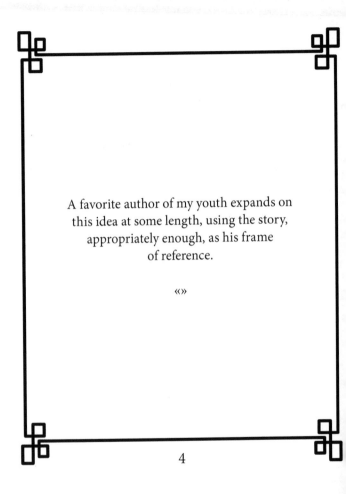

A favorite author of my youth expands on
this idea at some length, using the story,
appropriately enough, as his frame
of reference.

《》

The author of this classic novel of politics
offers advice about how to know oneself.
Having read this novel relatively recently,
I found that it contains so much more—
a love story and a saga of maturation.

《》

*(It is human defect—to try to know oneself
by the self of another. One can only know
oneself in God and in His great eye.)*

Robert Penn Warren, *All the King's Men*

This highly esteemed, Nobel Prize–winning author suggests that some people may make a conscious effort to achieve isolation from others.

«»

We're usually waiting for somebody to clear out and let us go on with the business of life (to cultivate the little obsessional garden).

Saul Bellow, *The Dean's December*

Now, we confront the important and recurring questions of if and why we should care about others.

«»

For who, in his heart, really wants to give much of his time to another man's concerns?

Robertson Davies, Leaven of Malice

The same question is asked here, but with a particular emphasis on this male character's disdain for women, which was caused by his very bad experience with marriage.

《》

Why should anyone care about other people? Let everybody keep their feelings to themselves, as he would his. Especially about women!

D. H. Lawrence, John Thomas and Lady Jane

Using a telling simile, this English novelist and philosopher asks if we can ever know ourselves, a very fundamental question, to be sure.

«»

"Imagine what the world would be like if there were no mirrors....But where our personalities are concerned, most people are living in a world without mirrors."

Colin Wilson, The Personality Surgeon

We will end this section on a "high note," that is, with an admonishment to be unselfish.

《》

Everybody forgets. We should all be kind and good and unselfish if we always remembered—remembered that other people are just as much alive and individual and complicated as we are, remembered that everybody can be just as easily hurt, that everybody needs love just as much, that the only visible reason why we exist in the world is to love and be loved.

Aldous Huxley, *Those Barren Leaves*

Alone
Without Meaningful Relations

To be, or not to be, alone? Do we have a choice? Is it only a state of mind? In either case, is loneliness the same as being alone? What are the benefits and detriments of being alone? Do you believe the benefits of your close relations outweigh the burdens? How do we feel when we are, or sense we are, alone? Why do some people prefer to be alone while others seek relationships? These quotes address some of these questions.

This very successful and popular Southern author contrasts the apparent culture of a Southern state with that of a Northern one to advocate a benefit of avoiding interaction with others, at least strangers.

«»

In Louisiana people still stop and help strangers. Better to live in New York where life is simple, every man's your enemy, and you walk with your eyes straight ahead.

Walker Percy, *Love in the Ruins*

A prolific, popular novelist describes some of the downsides of relations, at least for older people.

«»

All in all, being [alone] without any need to play a role was preferable to the friction and agitation and conflict and pointlessness and disgust that, as a person ages, can render less than desirable the manifold relations that make for a rich, full life.

Philip Roth, *Exit Ghost*

Should we question the assumption, underlying this quote, that we can be alone when we are physically with others? Note the character's interesting and ironic preference.

«◇»

"Solitude is a condition best enjoyed in company....Especially the company of one other soul,...It's dreadful to feel alone and really be alone. But I love to enjoy the feeling when I'm not."

Eleanor Catton, *The Luminaries*

Here is a very forceful argument that
we are always and necessarily alone.
The metaphor at the end is quite evocative,
and one that may be hard to forget when
we are passing by a herd.

《》‹

Because they were alone. In fact everyone was alone all the time, but when you got sick you knew it, and that was a lot of what suffering was—knowing....

It was good to be alone. Really alone, without other people around to let you imagine that your life had mingled with theirs. That was never true. Even together, people were as solitary as cows in a field chewing their own cud.

Tobias Wolff,
"Migraine"
in *The Night in Question*

Being alone may, however, create some
serious internal discomfort and anxieties.

«»

*Because being alone was dangerous. There
were no barriers to deflect an idea, no voices
to draw out the one thrumming in his head,…*

Lawrence Thornton, Naming the Spirits

Feeling or physically being alone may be a disadvantage for those people who are seeking not to be alone.

«»

Experience had taught them both that it was better to be with a mate in order to catch or attract another mate than to be alone. Alone was undesirable, vulnerable; alone put you in a weakened position.

Dan Wakefield, Starting Over

The sense and displeasure of being alone may be exacerbated when one sees others, especially couples, together. The metaphor at the beginning of the last sentence works for me, but I have not spent enough time in the kitchen to appreciate the "too many cooks…" allusion.

《》

In general, he was appalled by the various duos: Butch Cassidy and the Sundance Kid, Bonnie and Clyde, the Reagans. He looked around him and all he saw were these duos. It was like needing the prescription changed in your reading glasses; the world was made incoherent by duos or by people trying to cook side by side.

Thomas McGuane, *Keep the Change*

If you would like a more concise
expression of the idea, here is one.

«◊»

*...Like most lonely souls, he saw happy
couples everywhere.*

Eleanor Catton, The Luminaries

Is this advice too skeptical, even cynical?
If not, it is quite a strong admonition to
keep one's distance from other people.

«»

*Oh, it's the closeness that does you in. Never
get too close to people....*

Anne Tyler, *Dinner at the
Homesick Restaurant*

I found this advice very astute because it is far too easy to avoid asking why someone is alone. If we were to ask, we might treat people we find alone more compassionately.

《》

The reasons for seclusion were many. One should find out why a man is alone before one lets him alone, for he may not want to be alone.

        Elizabeth Goudge, The Dean's Watch

So, even if some people appear to have close relations, appearances may be deceiving.

«»

"Nonsense, he doesn't have any friends. All he has is useful acquaintances. He has a system of mutual advantages, but no friends. Nobody has six real friends."

John Hersey, *The Marmot Drive*

Adverse Factors and Relations

It is an oversimplification to suggest that relations fall into two general categories—good and bad. There are, of course, some or many with a mix of favorable and unfavorable characteristics. It will probably come as no surprise that many authors of literary fiction devote more attention to negative relationships than to positive ones. Maybe there is only so much that can be written about blissful relations if the author wants to have a commercially successful novel. Hence, here are quite a few illustrative quotes.

Let us start with a relatively mild adverse relationship and personal traits that should eliminate it. It is fun to start the section about negative relations with a quote from an author who is well-known for his sense of humor.

«◊»

A host can always solve the problem of the unwanted guest if he has a certain animal cunning and no social conscience.

P. G. Wodehouse, A Pelican at Blandings

The lack of a bona fide close relationship described here applies to many more than the two classes of people that are the subject of this quote.

«»

As with any celebrity or politician, the man was your best friend until the next time around when he has no recollection of ever having met you.

E. L. Doctorow, *Homer & Langley*

One can, apparently, become cynical about what others have to offer. Viewing what they have to say with disdain is unlikely to create favorable impressions.

«»

After a life rich in emotional defeats, I have looked around for other modes of misery, other roads to destruction. Now I limit myself to listening to what people say, and thinking what pamby it is, what they say.

Donald Barthelme, Snow White

The next few quotes identify some indicators of negative relations. The first one makes an ironic point.

«»

Because other people's weakness can destroy you just as much as their strength can. Weak people are not harmless. Their weaknesses can be their strength.

Philip Roth, Indignation

This idea resonates with me because of how I have often worried about our kids and let it show.

«»

...The person doing the worrying experiences it as a form of love; the person being worried about experiences it as a form of control.

John Lanchester, *Capital*

Here is a description of more
complications with worry, emphasizing
the burdens of the "worry-wart."

《》

But if the worry is about somebody else,
that's the worst kind. That's real worry
because if he won't tell you, you can't get
inside of the other person and find out why.
You don't know where's the switch to turn
off. All you do is worry more.

Bernard Malamud,
"My Son the Murderer"
in *The Stories of Bernard Malamud*

Fools, except perhaps in Shakespeare's tragedies, do not usually make good relations.

«»

He had made a fool of himself, but in good hands one does not mind.

Thornton Wilder, *The Woman of Andros*

This quote captures a common phenomenon that can poison otherwise favorable relations.

《》

"When people tell you to count your blessings,...it means they're on to you. They've sniffed out the fact that you don't appreciate all they have done for you. And they resent that...."

Louis Auchincloss, The Scarlet Letters

Here is an expression of the same
sentiment, using an interesting simile
at the end.

«»

*Whatever people gave you from their
overflowing hearts they remembered, and
expected you to remember, forever....There
was no such thing as petty cash.*

Tobias Wolff,
"Migraine"
in *The Night in Question*

I expect there will be little debate about the deleterious effects of dishonesty. The description of the manners of delivering falsehoods is amusing.

«»

The fundamental dishonesty of adults never fails to amaze her, their assumption that you'll believe whatever they say just because they're grown-ups and you're a kid. As if the history of adults' dealings with adolescents were one long, unbroken continuum of truth-telling. As if no kid was ever given a reason to distrust anyone over the age of twenty-five….Most adults prefer to expel untruths with little burplike coughs behind their hands, while others chuckle or snort or make barking sounds.

Richard Russo, Empire Falls

Here is a subtler take on dishonesty
that also focuses on how older people
treat children.

《》

*Grown people were always on the edge of
telling you something valuable and then
withdrawing it, a form of bully-teasing.
(Little of what they withdrew had any
value, but the pain of learning that can
be unpleasant.)*

Lillian Hellman, Pentimento

The absence of this ability to deal
with others can doom relationships,
but it is something with which many
of us struggle.

《》

*We may have problems forgiving others,
or ourselves, because life herself has never
forgiven anyone a single minute's time.*

Jim Harrison, The Road Home

The next four quotes identify some
characteristics that one might not expect
to be impediments to good relations.
I have witnessed quite a few examples
of the first one.

«»

*...But he was a man whose success gave
him reason to suppose he was smarter than
most people.*

E. L. Doctorow, *The March*

The assumption here is that some have
more or much more than others, but,
maybe, it is a problem for everyone.

《》

"Money is a great bar to intimacy."

Louis Auchincloss,
"The Lotos Eaters"
in *Tales of Yesteryear*

I would not have thought of this one,
but it may apply to people with and
without style.

«»

*Style is mighty pleasant for those who benefit
from it, but maybe not always rewarding for
those who make and live by its necessarily
strict rules.*

Lillian Hellman, Pentimento

After some consideration, this one made perfect sense to me, but it is not something I would have suggested on my own.

«»

...Nonchalance is a form of elegance, when it demands much, and declines to reveal its source.

Eleanor Catton, *The Luminaries*

This is an example of a problem between people who have something that others do not, expressed by one of my favorite British authors.

«»

...You can't blame the innocent, they are always guiltless. All you can do is control them or eliminate them. Innocence is a kind of insanity.

Graham Greene, The Quiet American

The same author in the same book takes the concept a step further, using a vivid metaphor at the end.

«»

Innocence always calls mutely for protection, when we would be so much wiser to guard ourselves against it; innocence is like a dumb leper who has lost his bell, wandering the world, meaning no harm.

Graham Greene, The Quiet American

We might generally think of idealism as a positive characteristic, but it can create impediments to relations with those who do not "measure up."

«»

"That's the worst of being an idealist; you won't accept people as they are."

W. Somerset Maugham,
The Narrow Corner

If we discover the absence of this trait in someone, the relationship may be doomed.

‹›

When kindness has left people, even for a few moments, we become afraid of them, as if their reason has left them.

Willa Cather, My Mortal Enemy

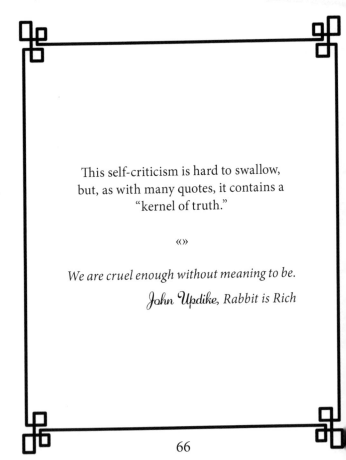

This self-criticism is hard to swallow, but, as with many quotes, it contains a "kernel of truth."

《》

We are cruel enough without meaning to be.

John Updike, Rabbit is Rich

The next two quotes reflect strong
condemnation of betrayal.

«»

*The world can accommodate many sincere
opinions but has no lasting use for turncoats.*

John Updike, *In the Beauty of the Lilies*

This one is even more disparaging than
the prior one.

«»

"You won't grow up until you learn that all
human beings betray each other and that
we are going to be let down even by those
we trust the most. Especially by those we
most trust."

Madeleine L'Engle,
A House Like a Lotus

Hard to imagine a more damning and thorough assertion about social relations than this one—quite a litany!

«»

"...Man is a social animal, characterized by cronyism, nepotism, corruption, and gossip."

Carlos Ruiz Zafon,
The Shadow of the Wind

We might well think that people who are enemies have developed the worst possible relations.

《》

...And when fighting in the dark one's enemies seem more monstrous than they really are. Knowing that they exist, but never seeing them face to face, makes one suspect that they are hiding behind every shrub.

Piers Paul Read, *A Season in the West*

There might, however, be an upside, a proverbial "silver lining." I hope you like the irony here as much as I do.

«»

...He liked his enemies best because he never had to doubt their sincerity;...

$\mathcal{E}than\ \mathcal{C}anin$, America America

How we develop a very favorable relationship may turn out to be how it deteriorates. Can you think of examples?

«»

Perhaps they had become enemies for the same reason they had once been friends.

Cormac McCarthy, *Cities of the Plain*

Hate is about as bad as a relationship can get, but it can be mixed with positive emotions. This quote expresses the conflicting emotions quite succinctly.

«»

"...You can hate a person with all your heart and soul and still long for that person."

Joseph. Mitchell,
"Joe Gould's Secret"
in *Up in the Old Hotel*

Here is a very thorough description of the negative consequences of having enemies and a sound suggestion of a way out. I like the simile toward the end.

«»

He knew that our enemies by contrast always seem with us. The greater the hatred the more persistent the memory of them so that a truly terrible enemy becomes deathless. So that the man who has done you great injury or injustice makes himself a guest in your house forever. Perhaps only forgiveness can dislodge him.

Cormac McCarthy, Cities of the Plain

One of my favorite contemporary authors identifies family issues that have crept out of the family and "poisoned the well" for other relationships.

«»

All jobs are surrogate families, complete with oedipal urges, sibling rivalries, and the ugly rest. The occupation and family, add primary social contact and recreational outlet. In another fifty years, we'll have returned to the medieval apprentice system, with parents selling their ten year olds into careers appointed by benevolent aptitude tests.

Richard Powers, *The Gold Bug Variations*

Parents' concerns for their offspring
know few limits, and disappointments
can be devastating.

«»

A son or daughter who travels at a wayward
angle must seem a penalty the parents must
bear—but for what crime?

Don DeLillo, Zero K

This character finds even a generally positive relationship full of ill effects. What a pessimistic conclusion!

《》

He disliked all burdens of responsibility, most especially when those responsibilities were expected, or enforced—and friendship, in his experience, nearly always devolved into matters of debt, guilt, and expectation.

Eleanor Catton, The Luminaries

This idea was a surprise for me. Does it apply generally or only to certain dressers or observers?

«»

It's a mistake to see people dressing. One should see them either dressed or naked; those are the only two decent states. All else is shame and disillusion.

Robertson Davies, *Tempest-Tost*

To conclude this section, we have a suggestion for avoiding having an apparently favorable trait become a deterrent to positive relations.

《》

The few intelligent people who truly wish to be liked soon learn, among the disappointments of the heart, to conceal their brilliance. They gradually convert their keen perceptions into more practical channels—into a whole technique of implied flattery of others, into felicities of speech, into euphemisms of demonstrative attention, into softening for others the crude lines of their dullness.

Thornton Wilder, *The Cabala*

Impossible to Know Other People

It may be reasonable to conclude that the reason, or, at least, a very important reason, for so many negative relationships is that we do not and, maybe, cannot, know other people. The assumption is that if we knew and understood them, we might, at least in some cases, develop favorable relations. (Another implicit assumption is that we know ourselves and are capable of making and sustaining close relationships.) The number of quotes on this topic indicates that it is a frequently offered explanation for difficulties in relationships.

My late uncle, with whom I often felt very close, used to say something like this frequently. One of my favorite contemporary authors states it so well.

«»

It's hard enough keeping track of ourselves. Once it comes to other people, we don't have a clue.

Paul Auster, Leviathan

Here is another very simple explication
of the proposition.

《》

"We never rightly understand the existence
of another, do we?"

Ethan Canin, A Doubter's Almanac

This prolific and popular author suggests that our knowledge, absent a post-mortem, can be only "skin deep."

《》

...It is presumptuous for anyone to even pretend he can know what another person's interior is really like, short of an autopsy. The only thing we can ever know for certain is skin....

Gore Vidal, *Myra Breckinridge*

Here is another stab at the same idea,
emphasizing that even the exterior is
hard to discern.

«»

*Everyone's skin is so particular and we are
largely unimaginable to one another.*

Jim Harrison,
"Legends of the Fall"
in *Legends of the Fall*

It seems, according to this observation,
that there is no limit to our ignorance.

«»

*You could not ever know enough about
where real people came from.*

John Irving, *Avenue of Mysteries*

Not knowing or understanding others
is a serious problem, but it is worse if
we think we do.

《》

*Always a mistake, to suppose that you know
what's going on inside anyone else's head.*

David Lodge, *Thinks...*

The principle of unknowability seems to apply even to family members, in this case because of interference from the self.

«»

You live beside people—strangers. She was so caught up in her life, she couldn't see her life, circumscribed as it was by that most inscrutable of mysteries—a family—where each of us understands everything and nothing at once.

Brad Leithauser,
The Art Student's War

So, does this mean we should give up?
I find this quote too pessimistic.

«»

*I simply found out that you couldn't know
another person's life, and might as well not
even try.*

Richard Ford, *The Sportswriter*

Here is a call for us to keep trying despite
the apparent futility.

《》

*Time has its revenges, but revenges seem
so often sour. Wouldn't we all do better not
trying to understand, accepting the fact
that no human being will ever understand
another, not a wife a husband, a lover a
mistress, nor a parent a child? Perhaps
that's why men have invented God—a being
capable of understanding.*

Graham Greene, The Quiet American

One reason for our failures to understand others is that we all change from time to time, sometimes for better, sometimes for worse. Again, we have a reminder of the risk of thinking we know others better than we do.

«»

But it was a nice way of ignoring another simple truth—that people changed, with or without wars, and that we sometimes don't know people as well as we think we do, that the worst errors in judgment often result from imagining we understand what has escaped us entirely.

Richard Russo, *The Risk Pool*

Perhaps, we have been misled into thinking that we are more alike than we are, and this misunderstanding contributes to our inability to understand others.

《》

The point is we are all quite different, and everyone tells us we're not. There is this inescapable, incredible variety of perception and sensation, the little parcels of experience that add up to a whole not necessarily typified by any sort of symmetric unity, but the urge of life herself.

Jim Harrison, Sundog

This quote uses a simile drawn from what we often need to have to be able to use modern systems, equipment, vehicles, and gadgets.

«»

She had been an education in the truth that people did not, in practice, come with a user's manual.

John Lanchester, *Capital*

This quote, however, uses some similes that hark back to the past, and ends with very heavy metaphor.

«»

In general, people were not road maps. People were not hieroglyphs or books. They were not stories. A person was a collection of accidents. A person was an infinite pile of rocks with things growing underneath.

Lorrie Moore,
"What You Want to Do Fine"
in *Birds of America*

Some of our problems stem from not distinguishing fact from fiction in others.

«»

There is truth and then again there is truth. For all that the world is full of people who go around believing they've got you or your neighbor figured out, there really is no bottom to what is not known. The truth about us is endless. As are the lies.

Philip Roth, The Human Stain

So, it seems that no matter what the other person is experiencing, we cannot peg it accurately.

«»

For the outsider—and everyone in this world is an outsider in relation to everyone else—something always seems worse or better than it does for the one directly concerned, whether that something is good luck or bad luck, an unhappy love affair or an "artistic decline."

Heinrich Böll, The Clown

According to this assertion, regardless of how close we think we are to others, we lack sufficient knowledge despite important common ground. The metaphor used for our not understanding strangers is quite creative.

«»

Men lived with their nearest and dearest and knew little of them, and strangers passing by in the street were as impersonal as trees walking, and all the while there was this deep affinity, for all men suffered.

Elizabeth Goudge, The Dean's Watch

No matter how close we get, we lack the
clarity we would like or need.

《》

*The deeper life between two people I had
yet to read with confidence. It seemed a
kind of vaporous text that kept revising its
very alphabet.*

Lorrie Moore, *A Gate At the Stairs*

The closer we get, the more likely we may be to overestimate our understanding or find that it does not serve us so well as we hoped.

«»

Knowing someone so well that you could anticipate their response to most things should make their responses easier to bear but in practise often does the opposite.

John Lanchester, Mr. Phillips

We conclude this section with a rather lengthy and thorough exposition of the issues. Note the usefulness of the military allusions.

《》

You fight your superficiality, your shallowness, so as to try to come at people without unreal expectations, without an overload of bias or hope or arrogance, as untanklike as you can be, sans cannon and machine guns and steel plating half a foot thick; you come at them unmenacingly on your own ten toes instead of tearing up the turf with your caterpillar treads, take them on with an open mind, as equals, man to man, as we used to say, and yet you never fail to get them wrong. You might as well have the brain of a tank. You get them wrong before you meet them, while you're anticipating meeting them; you get them wrong while you're with them; and then you go home to tell somebody else about the meeting and you get them all wrong again. Since the same generally goes for them with you, the whole thing is really a dazzling illusion empty of all perception, an astonishing farce of misperception. And yet what are we to do about this terribly significant business of other people, which gets bled of the significance we think it has and takes on instead a significance that is ludicrous, so ill-equipped are we all to envision one another's interior workings and invisible aims? Is everyone to go off and lock the door and sit secluded like the lonely writers do, in a soundproof cell, summoning *people out of words and then proposing that these word people are closer to the real thing than the real people that we mangle with our ignorance every day? The fact remains that getting people right is not what living is all about anyway. It's getting them wrong that is living, getting them wrong and wrong and wrong and then, on careful reconsideration, getting them wrong again. That's how we know we're alive: we're wrong. Maybe the best thing would be to forget being right or wrong about people and just go along for the ride. But if you can do that—well, lucky you.*

Philip Roth, American Pastoral

One of the Difficulties: Pretense

We should explore the reasons why knowing and understanding others is so difficult. Are we all guilty of putting on an act or playing a role that obscures our genuine personality? If so, does doing so improve or decrease our chances of our having long-term, positive relationships? Although many of us were encouraged to pretend when we were young kids, pretense is often not conducive to good relations between adults, even if everybody seems to be doing it and many of us recognize it when others do it.

We will start with some ideas about the
audience for our pretenses. The first
quote is a powerful statement about who
is, at least, first. We might argue that
after ourselves, pretending to others will
naturally follow.

«»

*We are only ever pretending to ourselves,
never to other people.*

Jose Saramago, The Cave

I am more inclined to favor this quote
over the prior one.

«»

*It was part of his power that he was so fine
an actor that he could convince himself as
well as others.*

Elizabeth Goudge, *The Dean's Watch*

The author of some highly esteemed
mysteries suggests a plausible fault
with self-deception.

«»

*"One deceives oneself you know. One thinks
that one wants to be understood when one
wants only to be half-understood. If a person
really understands you, you fear him."*

Eric Ambler, A Coffin for Dimitrios

When pretense appears exaggerated,
others may draw a conclusion contrary
to the pretense.

«»

"*I don't trust people who say they have a
lot of friends. It's a sure sign that they don't
really know anyone.*"

Carlos Ruiz Zafon, *The Angel's Game*

So, a little pretense may go a long way because (as suggested in the last quote of the next section) the audience is not so thoroughly engaged as we assumed.

《》

What he'd learned in the navy is that all you have to do is give a pretty good and consistent line about yourself and nobody ever inquires, because no one's that interested.

Philip Roth, *The Human Stain*

Here is another reason not to overdo the act, that is, because the audience may do a lot of the work "filling in the blanks."

«»

The shell of illusion needed behind it only a certain poise, a stillness, for the audience to feel engaged; it was better, in fact, not to reach out too boldly, but to allow the audience, like any object of seduction, the space in which to come forward and exercise its own volition.

John Updike, In the Beauty of the Lilies

We should acknowledge a potential
benefit of a well-executed pretense.

«»

*"One nice thing about keeping up a good
reputation, you never know when it'll come
in handy."*

John O'Hara, The Instrument

Here is another potential advantage of
"playing the game."

«»

*If you go along with how a person sees
you, then you learn a great deal about
that person.*

Doris Lessing, love, again

Pretending something of social value
may foster good relations.

《》

*The appearance of cooperation was worth
a great deal, if only because it forced a
reciprocity, fair met with fair.*

Eleanor Catton, The Luminaries

In some cases, pretense can benefit not just the pretender but also the people for whom the pretense is made.

«»

We know now that she was only pretending to be strong—which is the best any of us can do. Of course, if you can pretend to be strong all your life...then you can be very comforting to those around you. You can allow them to be childlike now and then.

Kurt Vonnegut, *Palm Sunday*

If the mask is removed, however, the consequences for the pretender and his or her audience may be serious.

«»

It is not good to see people who have been pretending strength all their lives lose it even for a minute.

Lillian Hellman, Pentimento

Another Difficulty: Effects of Others

It is always easy to blame others for our unsatisfactory relations, but we should keep in mind that we are "others" to them. Nonetheless, our perceptions of, and reactions to, others seem to have positive or negative effects on our relations with them. How important are others to us? How important should others' perceptions of us be? Is the effect on us of others' perceptions more often positive or negative?

We will start with what I hope will be a noncontroversial assertion about a benefit of taking others' perceptions into account.

«»

All agreements are founded on the proposition that at the end of the day it doesn't pay to be known as someone who is utterly perfidious.

Tom Wolfe, *A Man in Full*

Our reaction to others' faults may "come back to bite us."

«»

There seems to be a rule that what you condemn will turn up sooner or later, to be lived through....Beware of condemning other people, or watch out for yourself.

Doris Lessing, love, again

The character in this story finds lots of faults with relations with others—surely an exaggeration or product of some very unfortunate experiences.

«◇»

...Other people muddied the water. What with their needs and their demands and their feelings, their almighty anxieties to be tended to eight or nine times a day, you ended up telling so many lies that in time you forgot what the truth sounded like.

Tobias Wolff,
"Migraine"
in *The Night in Question*

128

To some extent, this quote takes us back
to the quotes in the first section about the
predominance of the self.

«»

*What right have people to make an image
after their own heart and force it on you and
be angry if it doesn't fit you?*

W. Somerset Maugham,
The Narrow Corner

Here is a form of vulnerability that others may exploit.

«»

The world is full of people who believe they never had their due, and they are the slaves of anyone who seems likely to make this deferred payment.

Robertson Davies, *Tempest-Tost*

We may overestimate our own powers and underestimate others' abilities. The author uses an excellent simile to make his point.

«»

Once more he had discovered that even when you have a sinner exactly where you want him, he still may have something to say; that it is, perhaps, a mistake to rehearse a play without inquiring whether your opposite is going to have some lines also.

Sinclair Lewis, *The Prodigal Parents*

A lack of tolerance for human frailty, of which there is plenty to go around, will make positive relations difficult.

«»

They wanted genuine intimacy, but they could not get even normally near to anyone, because they scorned to take the first steps, they scorned the triviality which forms common human intercourse.

D. H. Lawrence, Sons and Lovers

Don't you hate it when people do
not respond to you the way you want
and expect?

«»

*Unconsciously, perhaps, we treasure the
power we have over people by their regard
for our opinion of them, and we hate those
upon whom we have no such influence.
I suppose it is the bitterest wound to
human pride.*

W. Somerset Maugham,
The Moon and Sixpence

This author's conclusion seems very pessimistic. It cannot be true in all cases, can it?

«»

It's just heartbreaking that if you're nice to people, if you're reasonable, if you're modest, they tread all over you.

Philip Roth, *The Counterlife*

You may think you have successfully hidden part of your character, but you cannot be sure. What a great metaphor, at least for people who are handier than I am.

«»

You're like a nailhead that's been painted over. You think you're all covered up, but I can still see you under there.

Wallace Stegner, Recapitulation

Well, I suppose one person's vice might be
a virtue for someone else.

《》

"I've always believed,...that shamelessness
is your only virtue."

Gabriel García Márquez, In Evil Hour

Sometimes "calling a spade a spade"
will backfire.

《》

*No man likes to be called a coward—
and least of all, a man who is feeling
downright cowardly.*

Eleanor Catton, The Luminaries

It is appropriate to conclude this section with two competing observations about others' interest in us. Do you buy this one?

《》

...People were out there ready to think about you if you gave them the chance.

David Carkeet, Double Negative

Or this one, which I like very much and have begun sharing in conversations.

«»

We wouldn't care so much what people thought of us if we knew how seldom they did.

John Lanchester, Mr. Phillips

Positive Factors and Relations

Do you tend to "save the best for last" in some situations, or is it only some of us, or only me? Authors of literary fiction, or at least those I read, may be more interested in the flaws in human relations, their causes and consequences, than in the joys and rewards of positive, close relationships. Nonetheless, it behooves us to count our blessings for the gratifying relationships we have. We may want to explore ways to create and sustain more of them.

It may be trite to say that some relations turn out better than others, but we end up alone, for better or worse, if we do not, with some discretion, try to build some sturdy bridges.

«»

There is trial and error in all relationships. Have courage. Sometimes we draw strength from one another. We don't always bleed one another dry, and the trick is caution.

William Kennedy, The Ink Truck

Paying genuine attention to the plight of others and their perspectives, and having some sympathy for them, may be a good start.

《》

...The usual result of looking at something from someone else's point of view is to see how much worse off they are than you.

Kingsley Amis, *The Folks That Live on the Hill*

Finding something fundamental in common with another person should help.

«»

Once a man begins to recognize himself in another, he can no longer look on that person as a stranger. Like it or not, a bond is formed.

Paul Auster, *The Music of Chance*

This quote may seem to state the obvious, but we may not always think this way.

«»

If you liked a man you would invariably get on with him; if you didn't feel easy with him he almost certainly felt the same way about you.

V. S. Naipaul, *Magic Seeds*

Even if our liking others is not genuine
or wholehearted, it may be necessary for
productive associations.

«»

*Liking other people is an illusion we have
to cherish in ourselves if we are to live
in society.*

John Fowles, The Magus

This contemporary American author offers a low-key assessment of the value of some contemplation:

«»

"Some day you'll learn that you can't have people exactly the way you want them and that a little understanding is all you need to make most people seem halfway decent."

Wallace Stegner, The Big Rock Candy Mountain

The following six quotes introduce some shared experiences that may be sources for good relations. The first quote contains two ideas (for the price of one).

«»

A secret always has a strengthening effect upon a newborn friendship, as does the shared impression that an external figure is to blame....

Eleanor Catton, The Luminaries

Two more come from a previously
quoted author.

《》

"*The closest bonds we will ever know are the
bonds of grief. The deepest community one
of sorrow.*"

Cormac McCarthy, All the Pretty Horses

Some commonly shared characteristics may have different effects at different times in our lives. I wonder about the veracity of the first part of this quote.

«»

...We were the same age which is as great a barrier to friendship among the young as it is an invitation to comity among the old.

Gore Vidal, Two Sisters

I confess that I am one of the "everyone" in this quote, having had some first-hand experience with the phenomenon.

《》

Everyone knows that, so long as the occasion lasts, there is no stronger bond of sympathy and good feeling among men than getting tipsy together. And how earnestly, nay, movingly, a brace of worthies, thus employed, will endeavor to shed light upon, and elucidate their mystical ideas!

Herman Melville, Omoo

This is one of the perceptive quotes
I collected from a recent reading of
this excellent novel.

«»

*The Friend of Your Youth is the only friend
you will ever have, for he does not really
see you....The Friend of Your Youth is your
friend because he does not see you anymore.*

Robert Penn Warren, All the King's Men

Having a significant problem in a relationship may lead to a significant improvement.

《》

"Happy are the associations," she would say, "that have grown out of a fault and a forgiveness."

Thornton Wilder, The Woman of Andros

Some people have greater capacity than others for this valuable contribution to their relations.

«»

There are some people you can forgive anything.

Patrick Modiano, Ring Roads

Is this true for everyone and every situation, or a bit of a hopeful exaggeration?

«»

You couldn't withhold forgiveness forever,...

Richard Russo, "Voice"
in *Trajectory*

This is an important trait, and some people have more of it than others, and, in some cases, too much. The last two sentences offer us some words of wisdom.

«»

True loyalty is much more rare than anyone might imagine. All the more so since expressions of devotion are so commonplace and so easily gained. Loyalty seems to be so common because it is so seldom put to the test. But the test of loyalty is the only true definition of it.

George Garrett, *The Succession*

It is only fitting that we end with a general explanation of how beneficial positive relations are.

《》

...*Association renders men stronger and brings out each person's best gifts, and gives a joy which is rarely to be had by keeping to one's self, the joy of realizing how many honest decent capable people there are for whom it is worth giving one's best (while living just for one's self very often the opposite happens, of seeing people's other side, the side which makes one keep one's hand always on the hilt of one's sword).*

Italo Calvino, The Baron in the Trees

End of Relations

Like all other good things, this good relationship must come to an end. My collecting quotes on this and other topics will, however, continue. I publish on my Facebook page quotes on topics in my books that I collected after submission of the manuscript, often trying to relate them to an upcoming holiday or to the season.

I hope that my efforts here, and in *Ross's Novel Discoveries*, *Ross's Timely Discoveries*, and *Ross's Thoughtful Discoveries*, will lead to a long-lasting and mutually enjoyable relationship between us. My principal objective is to share my discoveries with as many people as possible, hoping that the quotes will be amusing, interesting, and thought-provoking, and, perhaps, arming readers with fodder for fun relations.

I would like to express my deep appreciation for Tyson Cornell's enthusiastic support and creative ideas for this third volume of my quotations, and for the hard work by all of the staff at Rare Bird, including Alice Marsh-Elmer for the development and execution of the excellent design, inside and out, of the book; Hailie Johnson; Julia Callahan; Guy Intoci; Jake Levens; and Sydney Lopez.

Thanks to Cara Lowe for the illustrations.